ACIPENSER

Green Lake Monster

RUSSELL SLATER

This is a fictional story intended for entertainment purposes only. No part of this book may be reproduced or transmitted in any form without the written permission of the publisher.

Peninsulam Publishing

www.peninsulampublishing.com

Publishing stories Made in Michigan

ISBN: 1495413322
ISBN-13: 978-1495413322

DEDICATION

This book is dedicated to my beautiful, incredible wife, and our amazing son, who help remind me to enjoy the simple things in life.

CONTENTS

Ac·i·pen·ser. noun \ ¦a-sə- ¦pen(t)-sər\. A genus (the type of the family Acipenseridae) of ganoid fishes that includes most sturgeons.

-"Acipenser." *Merriam-Webster.com*. Merriam-Webster. <http://www.merriam-webster.com/dictionary/Acipenser>.

ACKNOWLEDGMENTS

Many thanks to my outstanding friends and family for your endless support and encouragement. I appreciate your interest, excitement, and inspiration. Special thanks to my friend Jordan Richardson, for your selfless contribution of artistic talent in the design of the cover artwork. I also wish to express my gratitude to the great people who reside in the Green Lake area. This book would not have been possible without any of you.

CHAPTER 1

EDGAR'S SECRET

Edgar Elzinga hopped into the tiny boat with a grunt. He shrugged a twisted burlap sack from his shoulder and sat it gently on the floor. Arching his lower back, the sixty year old farmer heard the crack of several vertebrate. It took several moments to get his "sea legs;" he lost his footing repeatedly as he grew accustomed to the ebb and flow of the waves.

Taking great care to remain silent, Edgar settled onto the aluminum seat and carefully dipped the paddle into the water.

"Full moon tonight," the farmer whispered to himself as he stared skyward.

Edgar noiselessly and steadily progressed through the water. His shoulders hunched and his hat pulled low, the farmer knew approximately how many strokes of the paddle it would take to get to his desired destination. He wanted to be right over the deepest part of the lake; it was important for what he was about to do.

When the strain on his shoulder grew to be unbearable, Edgar paused briefly to catch his breath. He wasn't in the same shape he'd been in as a young man, and these late night boat trips were often felt in his arms and back the following day.

Licking his lips and staring at the star-filled sky, Edgar pondered the wisdom of what he was doing.

"It's *got* to be done," he whispered, his voice barely audible. "Got to get rid of it *somehow…*"

The farmer knew that there were proper ways to dispose of rBST, the artificially manufactured growth hormone he gave to his cattle. Those proper methods were accompanied by volumes of paperwork, special disposal fees, screenings, cross-checks and verifications – all things that Edgar didn't have time or money for. It took a genius just to understand the regulations, not to mention jumping through all of their bureaucratic hoops. Who had time for that?

A family connection with a private (unregulated, cartel-owned) laboratory in Veracruz, Mexico meant that Edgar regularly received parcels containing rBST vials through the mail. The fact that the "juice" was slightly past its recommended shelf life didn't affect its quality. It worked just fine. As it was intended. Since Edgar got the stuff at such a discount, he'd be a fool not to try to gain an edge on his competition.

He couldn't just throw the stuff out with his weekly garbage, though. The risk was too great. It was much easier to take the broken needles from botched injection attempts, used syringes, and partial glass vials and then bundle them into plastic food containers, thoroughly "sealed" with duct tape. He taped heavy rocks to such bundles to ensure they sank to the lake's bottom.

Occasionally the farmer felt guilty for what he did, but since the "growth juice" was approved for use in cattle, for eventual human consumption no less, he concluded that its presence in the lake posed no serious health risks. He couldn't just stop the rBST treatments; it made his normally average-sized steer into robust, record-breaking animals. The beef quality was top notch, and thanks to regular injections of rBST, always in abundant supply. The return on his investment had never been better. Why would he want to stop making unprecedented profits?

As Edgar's internal moral debate came to a close, he again picked up the paddle and slid it into the water. The late hour required absolute stealth on his part. He couldn't afford to attract the attention of any of the lakeside residents who might report his presence. Illegal possession of rBST came with a stiff fine and possible jail time. Illegally dumping rBST-tainted waste into a public body of water would certainly result in permanent confinement to a cell at Jackson State Prison if he were caught.

Having finally reached the ideal depth, Edgar delicately brought the paddle out of the water and laid it in the boat. His eyes swept the lakeshore, watching for movement and signs of life. The homes were dark, only an occasional backyard lit by exterior lights. The coast was clear. The farmer's perpetually dirty and cracked hands fumbled with the tied end of the burlap sack. He dug out each taped bundle, eight total, and lined them up at his feet. As he worked, he heard a subdued splash nearby.

Edgar's spine stiffened. He held his breath and looked around. Seeing nothing, he shrugged and returned to his task.

CRACKLE. CRACKLE. The old man's hearing wasn't as sharp as it used to be, but he unmistakably heard the odd crackling noise echo across the lake. It sounded like billiard balls colliding, or footsteps on a hard surfaced floor. He didn't recognize it as a normal sound, and the rising alarm he felt made his heart beat faster.

Edgar forced himself to ignore the odd sounds. He needed to finish what he started, *then* he could get the hell out of there (which the logical part of his brain urged him to do).

Working with renewed urgency, the old farmer lowered each bundle into the warm water and released them, one by one. Unbeknownst to Edgar, a long, slimy whisker emerged from the lake and groped the side of the aluminum boat, "feeling" the vessel curiously. After thoroughly exploring the riveted surface, the whisker slipped back into the water unnoticed.

Soaked with perspiration (from his exertions and heightened nervous state), Edgar dropped the final bundle and immediately started to paddle back toward shore. The dirty work was done for now.

CHAPTER 2

DESIGNATED SWIMMING AREA

"Come on, Buddy," little Billy Brush called out, slapping his thigh. Buddy, the Brush family's lean and muscular German shepherd, distractedly sniffed the base of a neighbor's mailbox that he'd marked with urine only moments before. "Buddy! I said *come!*"

The animal perked its ears and cocked its head to the side inquisitively. The incessant snapping of Billy's fingers finally motivated the dog to abandon his investigation and resume his obedient position at the boy's side.

Billy passed house after house with his canine companion, whistling a random tune. He absent-mindedly tossed a shiny blue Frisbee into the air and caught it as they strolled along. The boy's tossing excited the hyperactive German shepherd. Buddy repeatedly circled Billy as they walked, prancing on his hind legs and snapping at the Frisbee.

"Not yet," Billy scolded, wagging his finger at the family pet. "Down!"

They finally reached the gravel parking area that marked the easily overlooked entrance to the township park. It was a barebones, forty foot wide grassy patch, with a single picnic table, outhouse and sandy beachfront.

There were no signs or other identifying markers that could be seen from the road to welcome visitors. One had to journey down a lopsided two track between a pair of upscale houses before the weather-beaten sign for "Leighton Township Park" became visible. Confused out-of-towners were often hesitant to walk that far, fearful of treading on private property. For locals, it meant the tiny stretch of publicly-accessible lakeshore remained their best kept secret.

Billy was well aware of the secret, as well as many others. He'd spent the bulk of his nine years on or near Green Lake. He knew all of his neighbors in the tightly-knit community, and all of his friends lived within walking distance. He felt "at home" whether he was sitting on his front steps, playing basketball in the church parking lot or making s'mores in a neighbor's backyard. The rural northeast Allegan County neighborhood was his safe place, his comfort zone.

"Cool." Billy bent to examine a perfectly flat stone amongst the pebbles. "Good for skippin'."

The boy's words captured Buddy's attention. He trotted over to sniff at the rocks. He found the flattened stone to be completely uninteresting. The true object of his desire was the blue Frisbee tucked under Billy's arm.

Billy stood up, drew his arm back and pitched the stone at the serene greenish-blue water. It skipped perfectly three times before it disappeared below the depths with an audible "plunk." Billy watched the ripples dissipate, clouded by the early-morning mist that hung over the lake.

"Yes!" Billy exclaimed, raising his clinched fist in victory. His father had taught him the art of stone-skipping earlier in the summer. Many failed attempts later, little Billy Brush finally mastered the skill.

The anxious German shepherd nearly plunged into the water to chase after the stone. When he noticed his tiny master preparing to throw the Frisbee, he reconsidered.

"Ready, boy? Ready? Go get it!"

Billy whipped the Frisbee from the hip, sending the spinning plastic disk toward the cylindrical white buoys that bobbed along the perimeter of the designated swimming area.

Buddy instantly became a blur of brown and black fur as he raced after his prize. The beast hit the water with a tremendous splash, barely slowing his pace. He frantically paddled toward the buoy, eyes and snout just poking above the water. His teeth expertly clamped down on the floating Frisbee as he started to turn around.

"Now bring it back," Billy commanded from the shore, but Buddy didn't need to be instructed. This was their favorite game, and Buddy knew it well. The dog was already returning as Billy tested the water and waded up to his knees to meet him. The stubborn dog refused to relax his jaws as the boy tried to wrestle the toy away. This was also part of the game. "Buddy, *give it*."

Having triumphed over his pet in the test of strength (which Buddy intentionally lost), Billy assumed his throwing stance and belted the Frisbee even farther than he had before. Buddy once again displayed his amazing speed, returning with the firmly-held Frisbee in record time. This time he gave up the toy with little resistance.

"Mister hot shot, huh?" Billy inhaled deeply, summoned all of his strength and released the Frisbee with a snap of the wrist. Like a shiny blue UFO, the disk sailed smoothly through the air. It travelled over and beyond the farthest buoy and disappeared into the thick blanket of fog. Several more seconds passed as both dog and boy listened for its watery impact.

SPLASH!

Undaunted by the extra swim, Buddy leapt from Billy's side into the increasingly choppy waves. The boy wore a huge grin as he watched the dog paddle, slowly swimming past the buoys. It took another full minute before Buddy saw his floating blue target, a great distance beyond the swimming area.

The dog's boundless energy finally diminished as he neared the Frisbee, exhausted. Billy was winning the battle to tire his pet, but the boy's victorious smile soon faded when he noticed Buddy circling the Frisbee repeatedly.

"What are you waiting for?" Billy called out through cupped hands. "Get it and bring it back." The boy was perplexed by the dog's sudden hesitancy. Buddy looked around, nervously scanning the water. "Come on, you dumb dog. What's the matter with you?" The animal's eyes darted around. He ignored the Frisbee, whimpered and made a beeline to the safety of the shore. "*Buddy!* Go get your toy! Momma's going to be mad if we lose *another* Frisbee!"

The German shepherd ran past the boy and jumped onto the grassy shore. With ears back and still whimpering, Buddy noisily shook the water from his coat.

"Buddy, you chicken," Billy teased. "Go get the Frisbee!" The dog only whined his response. Billy sighed, crossed his arms and apprehensively peered out onto the misty water. "*Fine.* I'll go get it myself then!"

Billy stomped through the muck, wading into the lake until the water reached his chest. He sprang off the bottom and kicked his feet. He developed a renewed admiration for his pet as he realized the swim was actually much farther than it looked.

Passing the white buoys, Billy felt a twinge of nausea as he swam. He was breaking the rules. His parents always taught him to stay within the confines of the swimming area. They strictly enforced the rule when they were with him and fully expected him to do the same when left alone. They were always clear when they explained their motivation behind the rule; the water beyond that point was very dangerous. The apprehension turned to excitement the further he swam, eventually losing sight of the tiny park beach.

CRACKLE. CRACKLE. The dog took notice of the strange sound and began to bark.

"Shut up, Buddy," Billy choked, spitting out a mouthful of lake water. He didn't want his pet's barking to bring the attention of the neighbors. What began as a series of concerned yelps grew into a steady chorus of warning barks.

Billy breathed heavily as he halted to tread water. He swam in a circle, searching for the missing Frisbee. He wondered if it could be further out into the fog-cloaked lake. Should he turn back and admit defeat or keep going?

SPLASH. The desperate barking ceased while Billy squinted his eyes. What was that dog doing?

"Buddy?" Billy breathed quietly through his nose. All he could hear was *something* moving through the water. The boy suddenly felt very frightened. He *knew* he shouldn't have gone past those white buoys!

A pair of sharp barks broke the silence. Billy saw Buddy swimming toward him, eyes wide. The boy felt relieved to see his pet. Suddenly

9

feeling silly for being scared in the first place, Billy turned away and resumed the hunt for the Frisbee.

"There it is!" Billy squealed. He lowered his face into the water and kicked his feet. "Got it!" Billy held up the disk like a trophy, excess water dripping down his arm. "Buddy, look…" Billy turned to share the good news, but was shocked to find himself alone yet again. He looked around, confused as he felt the fear return. "Where'd you go? Buddy…?"

SPLASH, GASP! The German shepherd broke through the water's surface with force, released by something unseen down below. The dog half-choked, half-barked his distress, trying to regain his bearings. Billy's face registered his instant panic and he frantically swam toward the buoys.

"Come on, boy!" The disoriented dog followed in Billy's wake, eager to exit the water. Just as they passed between the buoys marked with orange words of warning, Billy shot a glance over his shoulder. He saw nothing strange.

With heart pounding, the boy slowed down once he was within the protection of the semi-circle outlined by the buoys. He could almost touch bottom. Almost safe. His mind raced with excited thoughts.

"What the heck…?" Billy huffed, frustrated. Buddy was nowhere in sight. Vanished, again. The wild swings of emotion from relieved confidence to panicked terror were taking their toll. Tears welled up and broke loose as Billy began to sob. His little fist punched an oncoming wave, the first angry release of an impending tantrum.

SPLASH. In a flash of activity, Billy saw the kicking hind legs of his dog sticking out of the water, thrashing desperately. The paws disappeared, yanked below the surface violently. A moment later, Buddy's face just barely emerged, his snout sticking straight up. Watery yelps of pain mixed with the splashing caused by flailing limbs.

Billy thought he caught a glimpse of *something*. It looked like a long, pointed fish tail, yet was much too big to belong to a fish. Was it some kind of eel?

SHFLOOP! The yelps were replaced by bubbles as Buddy was sucked under.

Billy turned and ran as fast as his legs could move through the water. He wailed at the top of his lungs, yelling for his mom, his dad... anyone who could help.

As his toes reached the sandy shoreline, something large hit Billy's legs and knocked him off balance. The skin that brushed by wasn't scaly like a fish, but felt slippery and smooth, like wet rubber.

"Help me!!" Billy screamed. A trio of hooked claws snagged the boy's ankles and tugged, pulling him off his feet. The water was only a few feet deep, yet Billy couldn't free himself from the ever-tightening grip. Kicking with everything he had, the boy's saucer-sized eyes briefly focused on the odd, wedge-shaped mouth bearing down on him.

The massive mouth bore no teeth; it had four whisker-like barbels, similar to a catfish. These appendages felt around the mucky bottom near Billy's bare toes, passed over the boy's legs and seemed to recognize a potential meal. The razor-sharp talons at the end of an awkwardly long and thin arm dug in, gripping the squirming child. The slit of a mouth opened wide.

Billy punched and gouged at the gargantuan, to no avail. Like a giant vacuum, the creature inhaled, pulling the boy into its mouth up to his waist.

"NOOO!!" The creature lifted its head vertically and opened its mouth wider.

GULP! The force of gravity coupled with another intake of air caused Billy to disappear from sight, sliding deeper into the velvety recesses of the creature's mouth and beyond. He was gone.

Swallowed whole, little Billy Brush joined the slurry of his pet's remains in the creature's churning pool of stomach acid.

The creature turned back toward the familiarity of deeper waters and scurried away. Pushed along by flapping fins and long, skinny limbs, the creature returned to the green depths and disappeared.

Calm replaced the recent turmoil. The waves resumed their normal choppiness, and the fog blanket slowly receded with the rising intensity of the sun. There were no signs of the recent trauma. Nothing out of place or strange... except for the floating blue Frisbee without an owner.

CHAPTER 3

THIS IS GREEN LAKE

An entire month passed since the tragic disappearance of William Brush and his dog Buddy. The local churches included his name at the top of their prayer lists, but few residents thought there was any real chance of locating the boy.

The nine year olds' parents, Frank and Cindy Brush, personally participated in exhausting search efforts on or near Green Lake. They posted Missing Persons posters all across Leighton Township and neighboring communities. They made tearful appeals for their son's safe return in front of news cameras. They did everything in their power to bring Billy home.

Long after the Allegan County sheriff's marine patrol called a halt to the fruitless search, Frank and Cindy remained vigilant. They questioned neighbors in the area, and scoured lakefront properties for any clues of their child's whereabouts. They were deeply pained by Billy's unexplained absence, but what hurt almost as bad were the quiet, implied accusations from lifelong "friends." Some openly questioned the parents' sincerity, and some even speculated that they themselves played a devious role in the boy's disappearance.

"Allegan County authorities are still seeking the public's help in locating nine year old William Brush, who went missing four weeks ago today near Green Lake, in Leighton Township," said the monotone radio broadcaster. The scratchy voice blared from the blown speaker of a radio sitting in the corner of the rickety pontoon. The reception cut in and out with the rise and fall of the waves. A frustrated hand thumped the old machine and adjusted the duct-taped antenna.

"Brush was last seen around seven a.m. on the morning of June 4th, walking along West Shore Drive with his German shepherd. The boy's mother, Cynthia Brush, reported her son missing later that morning when he and the family pet failed to return home. Local and state officials have turned up nothing after extensive searches of the area, and further efforts have been discontinued. Anyone with information on the missing boy's whereabouts is asked to contact their local law enforcement agency.

In other news… the forecast is hot, sunny and humid this Fourth of July weekend. With highs expected to reach the upper nineties, residents are encouraged to hydrate properly and seek shade…"

"Screw the shade," declared Solomon Baxter. The deeply suntanned and shirtless middle aged man spoke to his audience of four friends, each seated around the pontoon with drinks in hand. He swirled the last millimeter of beer around the nearly vacant can before tossing it overboard. "I *do* like that part about hydration, however. Tommy, throw me a new one, will you?"

14

"You ask me, Frank and Cindy sound like they have something to hide," opined Tommy Raab, as he dug two fresh beer cans from their icy home in the cooler. He threw one to his buddy, then cracked his own can and emptied a quarter of it in a single pull. "They probably buried the little guy under their front porch."

"Why the hell would they do that?" Shirley Baxter asked defensively. Like her husband, she was burnt to a brown crisp from overexposure to the sun. "You're drunker than I think you are if you honestly believe that. Frank and Cindy have lived around here for years. They're a good Christian family; we go to church with them. We just saw them at the free pancake breakfast and you didn't have anything negative to say! Just waitin' until their backs are turned, huh?

They've got enough of a burden to bear without people talking about them that way. You should be ashamed of yourself! How would you like it if something terrible happened in *your* family and your so-called 'friends' spread rumors about you?"

"You can never be too sure about people, hon," Solomon chimed in, taking his friends' side over his wife's. "Whenever they discover a serial killer, the neighbors always say the same thing. 'They didn't seem like the type... nicest people in the world,' and all that. How well do we *really* know our neighbors? Their tears might seem convincing, but guilty parents have done the same thing in the past. Remember that woman who said someone stole her car, with the kids in it, but it really turned out that she--"

"Shut up, Solomon," Shirley commanded as she released a belch that would make any man proud. Rediscovering a sense of modesty, she belatedly placed a hand over her mouth. "Excuse me."

"I don't trust them," Tommy said. "Something's just not kosher with their story. I can hear it in their voices."

CLUNK. Something hit the boat's underbelly, hard. The partiers pitched forward. Amid the cussing and spilled beers, a panicked uncertainty washed over the faces of the boat's occupants.

"What the *hell* was that?!" Shirley croaked as she recovered her foaming beer can.

"Not sure," replied her stunned husband. He, Tommy and a third male friend named Levie walked around the pontoon, and cautiously peeked over the edge into the water below. "I don't see anything."

"Maybe we hit a rock," said Cheryl, Levie's soft-spoken spouse.

"Not in *this* water," Solomon dismissed. "We're not close enough to the shore to hit any rock. Depth is probably around fifty feet right here."

"What else could it have been?" Shirley asked. "A log, maybe?"

"Nothing over here, either," Levie reported, peering over the tops of his sunglasses. "Whatever it was, it's gone now."

"Could it have been a fish?" Cheryl asked meekly.

"They shouldn't be *that* eager to get caught," Solomon chuckled. "Plus there's nothing in this lake big enough to hit us that hard. That was quite a jolt."

"We *have* been drinkin'…" Shirley trailed off.

"Felt like a great white shark rammed us," Tommy said with a grin, only half seriously. He imitated the theme from Jaws.

"Knock it off," Shirley said. "Of course it wasn't a shark; this is *Green Lake*, after all."

"As long as whatever it was doesn't come back, it doesn't bother me," Solomon shrugged as he returned to his up-turned bucket of a seat.

"You guys smell that?" Cheryl asked, sniffing the air. The rest of her friends smiled at her naiveté.

"Smells like someone's having a party," Tommy said. Cheryl looked confused.

"Pot, honey," Levie said simply. "Someone's smoking it."

"Stuff stinks," Cheryl observed with wrinkled nose. The others chuckled at her reaction. She stood, used her hand to shield her eyes and scanned the horizon. "I wonder where it's coming from…"

CHAPTER 4

GET OUT OF THE WATER

Silas Sobel sat in the uncomfortable folding lawn chair at the end of his dock. He used an ancient pair of binoculars to observe the crowded lake traffic. Copious amounts of alcohol were being consumed on nearly every vessel, a clear violation of the law. Given that it was the Fourth of July weekend, the local lake cop mostly looked the other way unless the partiers exhibited excessive behavior.

A veteran of the Vietnam conflict, Sobel's practice of observing the people and things in his environment had saved his life many times in combat. Now he utilized his skills to take mental notes on the habits of his neighbors. He considered it basic situational awareness. Not that any of it mattered, but it helped pass the time and old habits did indeed die hard.

Sobel lowered the binoculars, leaving circular imprints around his eyes, as he remembered the smoldering marijuana cigarette in his right hand. He brought the soggy-ended smoke to his lips and inhaled deeply. In his youth, deep inhalation almost always triggered a gag-inducing coughing fit, but now he expertly handled the lung expansion.

As Sobel exhaled a cloud of hazy smoke, his eye caught the movement of an approaching boat. It was the sheriff's marine patrol.

"Howdy," Sobel called out. "Happy Fourth of July."

"Same to you, Silas," the baby-faced deputy responded. He pointed to the special cigarette Sobel held between his fingers. "You know you're not supposed to be smoking that stuff outside of your home. We've been over this before."

"Get out of here, CJ," Sobel answered. Calling the young cop by his first name came with the familiarity of regular contact. "The State of Michigan gave me a card that said I can have this stuff."

"The MMMA says you have to consume your 'meds' indoors," the deputy said, referring to the state's ultra-controversial medical marijuana law. "And it's still illegal according to federal law."

"You a federal agent?" Sobel chuckled. "The feds can kiss me where the good Lord split me. I got *shot* on Uncle Sam's behalf; he can make an exception for me when it comes to smoking a little grass. If some VC hadn't shattered my leg for being in his country, then I wouldn't need this stuff to help the pain. Ever been in combat, CJ?"

"You know I haven't," Deputy Fischer replied. They'd been through this many times. Sobel always tried to guilt the deputy into leaving him alone. "That has nothing to do with it. I've got a job to do out here. Come on, Silas."

"Don't you have bigger fish to fry?" Sobel whined. "We've got dozens of drunks on the lake, and you're worried about my disabled ass. Give me a break!" He relented, and stubbed out the joint on his sandal.

"Thank you," Fischer said, relieved. "I appreciate your cooperation."

"I put it out because I've had enough for now," Sobel said forcefully. "Not because *you* told me to."

"Either way, thank you," Fischer persisted. "Just try to be a little more discrete in the future, will you?"

Sobel didn't answer, just stared at the deputy. Even forty years since he'd last tasted combat, Silas retained his thousand yard stare. Fischer wouldn't admit it, but he felt intimidated by the look. He turned the throttle on his outboard motor, and wordlessly left the area.

"Damn county mountie," Sobel muttered as he relit the medicinal joint. "I was killing commies for my country when his daddy was still in diapers." Puffing away happily, he brought the binoculars up to his eyes once again.

Sobel enjoyed living on North Lake Drive, although there had been more development in the area than he cared to see. What could one do? It was lakeside property, the demand for which had skyrocketed. His "section" of the lake was near the public access boat launch, but thankfully many boaters continued well beyond his dock for their fishing and recreation.

He watched the boaters speed around the lake in counterclockwise formations. Some towed teens on inner tubes while others narrowly missed the swarms of personal watercraft that buzzed through the water. Deputy Fischer had his hands full issuing citations and warnings to those who were having too much fun.

Shifting his view, Silas adjusted the position of his tingling leg. He rubbed the smooth mass of scar tissue just below his left knee. The 7.62 x 39mm round shattered his shin back in 1972, and despite years of surgery and rehabilitative therapy, the nerve damage was irreversible. The marijuana he consumed didn't kill the numbing ache, but it did soften its impact on his abilities to carry out daily tasks.

Sobel took one final drag before flicking the smoking remnant of the butt into the lake. With a sigh, he focused his attention back to the excited activity taking place on the water.

The scenes of good-natured laughing, drinking and smoking were repeated on each vessel. Everybody was having a good time.

One boat in particular caught his attention. It was a twenty four foot pontoon, similar to his own, floating roughly fifty feet away. Its occupants wore stunned expressions. Each held a beer, but they weren't laughing or joking. They looked deathly serious as three men edged their way along the boat, staring intently at the water below.

"What's got you fools spooked?" Sobel asked himself.

Without warning, the large pontoon shifted violently. The partiers aboard stumbled, took a knee or fell flat on their faces. Something big had hit the boat's bottom.

A foreboding feeling gripped Sobel's gut, similar to what he felt when going out on patrol in Vietnam. He was unfortunate enough to be picked for point man several times during his tour. During the eerie lull prior to an ambush, his stomach always tightened up the way it was doing at that very moment.

CRASH! Another strong impact raised the pontoon briefly out of the water. The people were now severely frightened. They congregated in the center of the craft, gripping each other or whatever else was solid.

Sobel fidgeted in his chair. What should he do?

Through the scratched lenses of the binoculars, he watched to see if any surrounding boats noticed the distressed pontoon. Nobody did. Everyone was too wrapped up in their own fun to notice anything amiss.

Several minutes of inactivity passed. The pontoon's passengers just gripped each other and waited. One of the men grew tired of waiting and cautiously stood up, inching his way to the side of the boat.

Sobel noticed movement in his peripheral vision. He watched a strange whip-like whisker appear from the water. It "touched" the boat's flank, exploring its shape and texture.

"What is *that*? A damn catfish?"

The whisker slipped back into the water. A million thoughts raced through Sobel's mind. Should he try to warn them? Should he call somebody? What was unfolding in front of him?

"HEY!" Sobel shouted. He coughed and cupped his hands. "HEY! There's something in the water!! Look out!!"

CRASH! Another hit. The brave (or stupid) man at the edge of the boat tumbled forward. The thin guardrail snapped like a twig when tested by the man's weight.

SPLASH. The panicked man tried to tread water as his friends rushed over to assist. Another man held out an oar for his buddy to take hold of.

"Help," the man croaked. "I need to get out of the water!"

Sobel watched, transfixed. His hand rummaged through his pockets, searching for the cell phone that he normally carried.

"Where the hell is it?" Sobel questioned. His hand turned up nothing but a book of matches and some lint.

CRASH! As if hit with a giant hammer from below, the pontoon rose several feet off the water's surface before plunging back down. This hit knocked the remaining passengers from the boat as they too joined the first man in the water.

CRACKLE. CRACKLE. A strange noise rang out. Sobel wasn't sure if someone's radio was amplifying the sounds of static, but that's what it sounded like.

Two of the bobbing heads instantly disappeared from sight, sucked under by some invisible force. The three remaining partiers swam away frantically, their pleas for help unheard by all expect for the watchful veteran.

"What the –" Sobel stammered.

Two more heads suddenly disappeared. The ripples in the water were the only signs of their recent presence. The final head, a male judging from the beard, spun around in a circle. He screamed, out of his mind with fear.

"Hold on, buddy!" Sobel shouted with the full force of his lungs.

SHFLOOP.

With that, the last head was gone.

CHAPTER 5

SOMETHING IN THE LAKE

S ilas Sobel nervously tapped his foot in the sand as he sat by his front door (the never-ending leg pain meant that he spent most of his time in a seated position). He was waiting for Deputy Fischer to stop by after his shift, which according to Sobel's watch, was nearly half an hour ago.

"Where is he?" Sobel asked with a cringe, struggling to find a comfortable position for his leg.

The veteran was very anxious. He wasn't sure what he'd just witnessed on the water, but he knew it was bad. He watched five people vanish in front of him without any ready explanation.

After the last man had been sucked under, Sobel raced inside the house as quickly as his bum leg would allow. He called the police, and insisted that the dispatcher notify CJ Fischer specifically. Silas didn't want to give his report to just any run-of-the-mill road patrol deputy. The slimy whisker he'd seen, the way the pontoon was rammed and the fact that the partiers were sucked under were all very odd occurrences. It would take a pair of trusted ears not to dismiss the story outright.

Another fifteen minutes passed before Silas saw the tan colored pickup bearing a sheriff's star pull into the driveway.

"Sorry to keep you waiting," Fischer said as he emerged from the driver's seat. "Been a busy day, as you can imagine."

"I've got something important to tell you, CJ," Sobel said boldly. The cop approached with clipboard in hand. The young deputy looked concerned. Sobel gestured toward a second vacant lawn chair close by. "Have a seat."

"What's up?" Fischer reluctantly lowered himself into the chair.

"There's *something* in that lake," Sobel said, pointing over his shoulder. "I saw it pull five people under the water." The deputy stared at him in silence.

"*What* did you see? Tell me exactly..."

"After I talked to you. Pontoon party about fifty feet northwest of my dock. Five middle aged adults. Three males, two females. They were drinking and having fun when they were suddenly rammed... something hit them and knocked them overboard. I saw them tread water before... *something* pulled them under."

"You saw them go under, but not come back up?" Fischer asked with growing concern. Sobel nodded grimly. "Christ, Silas! Why did you *wait* to report it?! They've probably drowned by now!!" The deputy jumped out of his seat and ran around to Sobel's backyard. He spat out specific details into the radio on his shoulder, relaying the information to the other marine patrol deputy who'd just relieved him.

25

Silas limped his way into the backyard where he eventually joined the sweating deputy.

"You won't find them," Sobel said matter-of-factly.

"Probably *not*," the excited cop replied. "Thanks to your failure to report it immediately. You said they were drinking, right? They were probably drunk, started messing around, fell overboard and drowned!"

"You're not listening! I said *something* pulled them under and never let go. They weren't drunk enough to drown as soon as they hit the water!"

"What do you mean, 'something' pulled them under?"

"The same 'something' that rammed their pontoon several times before it knocked them into the lake."

"Rammed them? Like an *animal* in the water?" Sobel nodded. "There's nothing out there big enough to ram a full-sized pontoon. Nothing's got the strength to knock five grown people into the water!"

"I can't explain it," Sobel shook his head. "There was *something* under their boat, CJ. I saw it."

"What did it look like?"

"I don't know. I only saw a weird-looking whisker."

"Whisker?"

"Like a catfish has. Only this one was... *bigger*; about as thick as my wrist and as long as my leg. Looked like it was feeling the boat. Like it was exploring... looking for something..."

Fischer raised a skeptical eyebrow. "You been taking more of your 'medicine' since I last talked to you, Silas?" He held his thumb and index finger together, brought them to his lips and loudly inhaled.

"Out on the dock. That was the last time I medicated," Sobel said irritably. "Why?"

"You know... it's just..." Fischer threw his hands into the air. "Look, I've known you since I started this job. I know you got hurt while serving your country and now you use an unconventional method to treat the pain. I'm okay with that, I really don't care if you want to smoke cannabis. But, what am I supposed to tell the sheriff?"

"The truth."

"What --? Should I say, 'hey boss, this pot-smoking Vietnam vet on the lake saw a giant catfish eat some people today?' See my dilemma? I can buy that you saw them drinking, fall in and never come out, and that's what my report will reflect."

"You don't believe me?"

"I really want to, Silas. I know you're not one to make up stories, but when it comes to lake monsters, seeing is believing. I can't pass wild claims up my chain of command without visual confirmation. Now, if you'll excuse me, I've got to help recover those bodies. Here I thought my day was almost over…"

Sobel hobbled back to his chair and watched Fischer drive away. Could he really blame the deputy for refusing to believe his story?

CHAPTER 6

NIGHT PAIN

CRACKLE. CRACKLE.

Silas sat up in bed with a start. His heart was pounding, his forehead moist and bed sheets sticky with sweat. The strange crackling noise sounded like that odd static he heard during the attack on the pontoon.

BANG! POW! CRACKLE. CRACKLE.

Looking out the window, Sobel saw brilliant flashes of light and vibrant colors before the sizzling, crackling sound. The fireworks show was in full swing.

Relieved, the startled veteran stretched out and closed his eyes, trying to catch his breath.

"If it's not one thing, it's another," Sobel groaned, rubbing his eyes.

He was referring to his perpetual cycle of nightmares about Vietnam; now they were about giant murderous catfish.

With the prospect of peaceful sleep quickly diminishing, Sobel scratched at his aching leg. It looked puffy and inflamed. His hands firmly massaged the badly-healed tissue, trying to restore normal circulation. After several minutes, he gave up and rolled over.

Silas plucked a tiny stub of a medicinal joint from the ashtray on his nightstand. He used extra care not to burn the tip of his nose as he got it going. Several deep drags later, the leg pain became slightly less noticeable.

Lying on his back, Sobel cleared his throat and stared at the squeaky ceiling fan that wobbled above. His thoughts again turned to yesterday's events. Could he have done more to save those people? *What was that thing he saw in the water?* That *thing* with whiskers, which produced that terrible CRACKLE sound, and apparently had an appetite for human beings. Did he really see it? Was he going crazy? Were more people going to die?

"I *know* what I saw," Sobel muttered confidently. But who would believe him? "I need to tell Bonnie Jean Buckingham. She'll know how to handle this."

Sobel nodded to himself as his eyelids began to sink. He finally drifted back into the land of slumber.

CHAPTER 7

THE MONTHLY MEETING

Together they pledged their allegiance to Old Glory, reciting the lines in practiced unison.

"...one nation, under God, indivisible, with liberty and justice for all. Please be seated."

Silas Sobel gratefully took his seat, thankful to relieve the growing pressure on his leg.

As the clerk rattled off the minutes of the township board's previous meeting, Sobel looked over his shoulder and scanned the miniscule audience in attendance. Spectators included himself, Fire Chief Terrance Techwyn, local journalist Ellie Donnovan, Deputy CJ Fischer, and William Jahnke, head of the residential association. They all took in the boring proceedings with polite silence.

While the seven-member board debated the merits of a rezoning recommendation, Sobel's steely blue eyes settled on the tough-yet-matronly supervisor, Bonnie Jean Buckingham.

Silas had known her since their graduation from Wayland High School in '71. Even after a failed romantic fling, the two remained close friends over the years. She was one of the few who kept up correspondence with him while overseas. He appreciated her kindness, admired her loyalty and was enchanted by her stern beauty. That's why he always chose her in the voting booth.

"… that takes care of the old business," Bonnie Jean proclaimed between sips of cold coffee. "Which brings us to public comment. Anyone have anything to say?"

Ellie Donnovan sat up and turned to a fresh page in her notebook. The young stringer knew that periods open to public comment were often the most interesting part of these sleep-inducing meetings.

"I've got something I need to say," Sobel raised his hand, ignoring the daggers being stared by Deputy Fischer.

"Go ahead, Silas," Bonnie Jean nodded, her voice warm and friendly.

"This might sound crazy, but it's the truth." A smile crept onto Ellie Donnovan's face. This should be juicy. "I saw something attack a pontoon full of people yesterday. It rammed their boat repeatedly. They fell into the water and were sucked under by something… *down below.*"

The board sat in stunned silence, unsure how to respond. The supervisor turned her attention to CJ Fischer.

"Do you know what he's talking about, CJ?" The deputy bit his lip and nodded.

"Yes, ma'am. Mr. Sobel gave me a full report of what he allegedly witnessed…"

"And...? Is it true?"

"We did find an abandoned pontoon," Fischer replied. "No sign of the boat's occupants. Mr. Sobel reported that he'd seen them consuming alcohol prior to their disappearance. We've yet to recover any bodies, but we're working on the assumption that they drowned because of their intoxication."

"That's *not* what happened," Sobel protested. "They didn't drown because they were drunk. They drowned because something large grabbed them and pulled them under." Bonnie Jean's greenish-brown eyes locked with Sobel's cold blues.

"What could it have been?"

"I don't know," Sobel admitted. "It was something *big*. Whatever it was, it looked to be at home in the water. Who knows? It could've had something to do with that little boy who went missing..."

A collective groan arose from the others in the room.

"Don't go there," William Jahnke whispered in warning.

The spunky journalist turned in her seat and looked up at the aging vet. "Ellie Donnovan, Green Lake Globe," the young woman introduced. "When you say 'something big' pulled them under, do you mean like a lake monster? Like Loch Ness?"

"That's not what I said..." Sobel sputtered.

"You can interview Mr. Sobel privately *after* the meeting," Bonnie Jean said, pointing a finger at Donnovan. "Do I make myself clear?"

"I'm just trying to get the story straight," Donnovan smiled deceivingly. She foolishly engaged the supervisor in a staring contest, which she promptly lost. "I'll discuss it with him later, though."

"I have a question for Mr. Sobel," began board member Peter Drake. "Now don't take offense to this, but your special 'meds' haven't been negatively affecting your better judgment, have they?"

"Up in smoke…," sang Mario Gulino, the trustee who owned the local pizzeria. The other board members snickered and laughed, with the exception of Buckingham. She thought the joke to be in bad taste.

"I don't want to hear another word about my 'special meds,'" Sobel replied, anger rising. "I'm sick of all the smirks and sideways stares. It's really none of your damn business anyway! I don't judge you guys for popping pharmaceuticals, do I?" He focused directly on Drake. "I don't judge *you* for drinking yourself stupid with a fifth of whiskey every Friday night, do I?" Drake's face turned red with embarrassment. His excessive drinking had caused him many problems, and his neighbors were well aware of it. "Smoking cannabis is the only way to relieve the 'dead log' feeling in my leg. The pain comes from a wound I received in Vietnam. Until they invent something that can actually help me without tearing up my guts or turning me into a zombie, I'll continue to treat my pain how I best see fit.

I'm trying to warn you about something dangerous out on that lake, and all you can do is pick on me or crack jokes?! *You're* the ones who're disconnected from reality! You'll see that I'm right… just wait."

With nothing else to say, Sobel tossed his copy of the agenda on the floor and made for the door.

"Silas, wait a minute," pleaded Buckingham. But it was too late, he'd had enough. The supervisor shot stares at the board members that could've melted glass.

Ellie Donnovan hopped up with notepad in hand and followed Sobel through the exit.

With a loud sigh, the cross-armed William Jahnke stood up and also left the meeting.

CHAPTER 8

STORIES OF LAKE MONSTERS

As Sobel limped toward his car, leg aching terribly, he sensed someone behind him. He stopped, pivoted on the sore leg, and confronted the nosy reporter.

"Mr. Sobel, can I have a few minutes of your time?" Donnovan chirped.

"I really need to get going home," Sobel answered with labored breath.

"It'll just take a minute."

Jahnke, president of the Green Lake Resident's League, took a standing position next to Sobel, casting a suspicious glare at Donnovan. "We don't want any trouble, young lady…"

"Who said anything about trouble? I just want to bring the truth to our readers," Donnovan smiled, adjusting her thick black-framed glasses.

"That's what I'm afraid of," Jahnke sighed, arms still crossed tightly. "Cooking up some sensational story is the type of trouble we want to avoid. If you'd please excuse us, Miss Donnovan... I'd like to speak to my friend in private."

"I haven't had a chance to ask any questions yet."

"You can get a hold of me sometime tomorrow," Sobel reassured, watching the smile melt from the journalist's countenance. "I'll tell you all about it. I promise."

"Fine," Donnovan relented. "I'll be in touch." She closed her notebook and walked briskly to her car. The men, intrigued by the sway of her skirt, watched her in silence.

"The media," Jahnke scoffed. "Always looking to stir up trouble."

"If she wants to write about what I saw, I'm not going to stop her. People *have* to be warned."

"Warned about what?" Jahnke's voice took on a confrontational tone. "We both know there's nothing out there. This is the biggest time of the year for the community. We've got the annual boat parade tomorrow. It draws a ton of business to the farmer's market, Mario's Pizza, the 3L store, Pham Vann's, the bowling alley... you name it. You don't want to go scaring folks away with crazy stories about lake monsters. There's *nothing* in Green Lake that isn't supposed to be there."

"I know what I saw, Bill."

"I prefer 'William,'" Jahnke enunciated.

"You do?" Sobel asked with mock surprise. "Well, Willy, I *know* what I saw. I wasn't having a 'Nam flashback, and I wasn't 'tripping' on my medicinal herbs, either. I saw something I can't explain *kill* five people. I don't want that to happen to anyone else!"

"You're not thinking clearly, Silas."

"I disagree, *William.* I'm going to do what I have to do."

Ignoring the man, Sobel finally reached his car and sat down. The vet closed his eyes and breathed a sigh of relief.

CHAPTER 9

ALL-SPECIES

"Morning, Jesse," Sobel said to the young clerk behind the counter. The Leighton Lakeside Landing, or "3L" to locals, was a small convenience store on the south end of Green Lake. Its limited staff of three employees was intimately familiar with their regular customers.

"Morning, Silas," the man replied, touching the brim of his camouflage cap.

"Slow day?"

"So far," Jesse admitted. "It'll pick up once church lets out and they get the boat parade under way." He peeked outside and noted that Sobel's pickup towed a pontoon on a trailer. "Going out on the lake today?"

"Yep," Sobel nodded as he scanned the snack rack. He'd taped a "GONE FISHIN'" sign on his front door that morning as he left, knowing that Ellie Donnovan would undoubtedly show up in person once she grew tired of unsuccessfully trying to reach him by phone. Despite what he'd told William Jahnke the night before, Silas really didn't care to discuss the details of the attack. For now, he'd had his fill of ridicule.

"What type of bait you looking to get? We've got minnows, crawlers, red worms, spikes..."

"What do you want for that?" Sobel pointed to a crusty, dried up chicken in the opaque rotisserie cooker, which badly needed degreasing.

"You don't want that," Jesse shook his head while making a sour face. "That's from yesterday. I've been meaning to throw it out. You don't want to eat it."

"Not for me." The clerk stared and thought for a moment.

"You want *that thing* for bait?" Silas nodded; Jesse laughed. "What the hell you looking to catch, a shark?"

"Maybe," Sobel answered evasively. "How much are you going to charge me for it?"

"I was just going to toss it," the clerk shrugged. "If you really want it, it's yours. Probably won't have much luck using it as bait though, unless you're trying to snag an alligator or something."

"Just throw it in a plastic bag for me." The clerk did as his customer requested.

"One day-old, nearly rancid chicken carcass... anything else for you today?"

"The pop, chips, candy... oh yeah, I need a fishing license too. Don't want to get into trouble with the DNR."

"Not a problem," Jesse smiled. "Just need your Michigan driver's license. Do you want restricted or all-species? Most guys go for the

38

restricted; lets you get everything except for trout, salmon, lake sturgeon, herring, amphibians, reptiles, crustaceans –"

"I need the *all-species* license..."

.

CHAPTER 10

A DAY ON THE LAKE

The setting sun cast a soothing orange/pink hue across the sky. Silas Sobel looked at his watch and sighed. With no luck and after enduring mocking comments all day over his use of deep-sea fishing equipment, he felt the urge to call it quits. It was a bitter-sweet feeling. He wanted to be proven right, to help stem any further threat to the safety of his community, but he was also afraid of what he might see. He already knew what the thing with whiskers was capable of. Maybe going home empty-handed wasn't such a bad thing.

"Not like the day was a total waste," Sobel shrugged.

Earlier that afternoon saw a tremendous congestion of lake traffic with the boat parade. Sobel was entertained by watching the spectacularly decorated boats of all sizes make their way around the lake, the stars and stripes and other patriotic banners flown with pride. Although he flew Old Glory from a pole in his front yard, he didn't feel compelled to dress up his boat like a grade school float. His mangled and barely-functioning leg was *his* display of love for his country.

Leading the flotilla was, predictably, William Jahnke (dressed as Uncle Sam), followed by vessels who advertised their local businesses in addition to the red, white and blue. Boats helmed by the owners of Mario's Authentic Pizzeria, 3L, Round Lake Bowling Alley, and Michelle's Bakery fell in behind Jahnke's cabin cruiser.

At the rear of the aquatic column was one of the town's most colorful characters, Pham Vann. He was the owner and operator of Pham Vann's Rental Store (which offered movies, sup pumps, rotor rooters, generators, and log splitters on loan). The cheery Vietnamese immigrant, who'd served in the pro-US Army of the Republic of Viet Nam, had waved enthusiastically at Sobel as he passed. Their acquaintanceship was an odd coupling in the small town, but they understood one another in a way that other residents never could. The two shared a common link to the past because both had fought for the same lost cause.

The parade aside, the day was rather uneventful. No boats rammed, no weird eggshell cracking sounds, no one pulled under the water, no sight of the bizarre, slimy whiskers.

"Damn, I guess my soggy chicken isn't good enough for *anything* out here."

Sobel checked his waterlogged bait periodically throughout the day. Smaller fish had nibbled away the darkened crusty skin, but it was otherwise untouched.

The soda pop, potato chips and chocolate bars he purchased that morning along with the unappetizing chicken were long gone. Sobel's stomach loudly protested its emptiness. He set the seven-foot long fishing pole to the side and unbuckled the special belt and lower back harness which focused the center of gravity around his hips.

"About that time, I suppose." Suddenly a peculiar, shrill sound pierced the air. Sobel's blood turned to ice.

CRACKLE. CRACKLE.

Sobel hastily re-donned the fishing harness and picked up the extra long rod in time to feel the first pull - an incredible tug that nearly yanked his shoulder out of socket. The black, one hundred-pound test line zipped from the shiny, massive reel at a dizzying rate.

"Hey... HEY...!!" Sobel screamed out to the few boaters who still lingered on the lake. They didn't notice his shouts, so he blared his foghorn for several long, drawn out blasts.

Sobel waited about thirty seconds before he locked down the reel, hoping that the giant hook would secure firmly in the mouth of whatever wanted to eat a whole chicken. As the thick line pulled taut, Sobel firmly planted his posterior in the metal alloy reel seat and braced his feet. This was going to be a hell of a fight.

"I need some help!" Sobel bellowed. "Can someone give me a hand?!" His shouting and repeated foghorn blares finally attracted the other boaters. He saw outdoor lights switch on in the yards surrounding the lake. The community slowly began to take notice.

The pontoon picked up speed, plowing through the waves as if being towed by a tug boat.

"This has *got* to be it," Sobel muttered breathlessly. The tugging finally subsided, the pressure on the line eased slightly. Sensing his chance to fight back, Sobel leaned back with all of his weight and reeled in the line just a little bit. He played a game of give and take, trying to hold the rod steady when resistance was strongest; when it relented, he took in as much of the slack line as he could.

"What the hell you got?!" asked an excited voice. Allowing the brief distraction of a leftward glance, Sobel saw the goofy, smiling face of Pham Vann approaching in his aluminum boat. "Godzilla or Frankenstein?" the immigrant laughed.

"Some... damn... *monster*," Sobel replied through clenched teeth. He fought with everything he had and already felt the early stages of muscle fatigue. In spite of the terrible leg ache, he stood up to get better leverage. "Give me a hand!"

The Vietnamese store owner let the bow of his boat gently bump against Sobel's larger craft. With rope in hand, Vann leapt onto the neighboring boat, tied off and ran to Sobel's aid.

"Here, give to me," Pham Vann said with confidence. He stood next to his friend, shoulder-to-shoulder, as his nimble hands reached over and grasped the rod. Both men leaned back simultaneously. "Damn! Feel like something out of rivers back home!"

As the pair who'd fought communism in their youth battled this new local threat, dozens of vessels converged on Sobel's location. Some, like Pham Vann, were participants from the earlier boat parade and still displayed their decorations. The veteran's drifting boat was eventually hemmed in on three sides by a constellation of curious boaters eager to see what was happening.

"We need more strength," Vann called out, partially obscured by his larger friend. "You all – come here and help us!"

Sobel was completely drenched in sweat. His left leg felt on fire and like it would give out at any moment, yet he persisted. More and more of the line was drawn back into the chunky silver reel, bringing whatever he'd caught closer to the surface.

The helpful neighbors crowded onto Sobel's boat, testing its holding capacity. Nearly every pair of hands that could touch the fishing rod were pulling along with Silas, grunting their exertions. Those who couldn't grasp the pole held onto Sobel himself, or someone who already had a firm grip on the man's harness. They added their weight to the efforts to gradually pull the line in.

Sobel was surprised to see William Jahnke, still in Uncle Sam costume, pull up in his own boat.

"So there's *nothing* in this lake, huh, *Will-i-am*?!" Silas managed a pained grin.

"What the hell's going on here?!" Few bothered to pay any attention to the demand coming from Deputy CJ Fischer. He and his flashing blue and red lights had arrived unnoticed.

"I THINK I'VE GOT IT, CJ…"

"Got *what*?!" the deputy asked, shining a high-powered search light into the water.

"That *thing*… with the whiskers!"

CRACKLE. CRACKLE.

The sharp-pitched shrieks grew increasingly louder. Whatever made such a noise was close.

SPLASH. A fin-like appendage broke through the surface, flapping wildly.

"There it is!" someone shouted. The fin disappeared and resurfaced several times. A lengthy, cartilaginous body thrashed violently, desperate to free itself from the hook.

"Come on!" Sobel urged his neighbors on. "Pull!! We've almost got it!!" Everyone leaned back at once, pulling the creature's colossal, wedge-shaped head briefly from the water.

"Holy cow!! Look at that *thing*!!"

The thick, whisker-like barbels, a pair on each side of its mouth, whipped around. A mammoth tail slapped at the surface, sending out powerful waves that threatened to capsize the smaller boats in the hodgepodge armada.

"Hold it steady!" commanded Deputy Fischer as he drew his sidearm. "Look out!" The excited residents saw the aimed weapon and backed away as instructed.

POP! POP! POP!

Three 9mm rounds hit their mark, just behind the beast's eye, but the animal only fought harder. Emitting an unearthly SCREECH of agony, it tried to dive back down, but the line pulled tightly and stopped its descent.

Mario Gulino, the young owner of the pizzeria, took aim with an old harpoon. Like an Olympic javelin thrower, Mario sent the spear sailing through the air, hitting the animal's humped back, near the spine. Another painful SHRIEK. More thrashing turned the lake into a bubbling cauldron of white-capped water mixed with blood.

The resistance on the line finally faded, the creature's extensive loss of lifeblood taking a toll.

"He almost out of gas!" Pham Vann yelled in triumph.

"Pull it up again," Deputy Fischer instructed.

Once more that strange, alien-looking head emerged from the churning waters, mouth opening and closing, its life nearly drained.

POP!

Fischer's last shot proved to be the creature's coup de grace. Its muscles twitched, an involuntary reflex of a failing nervous system, before the head peacefully sank into the water.

Silas Sobel, his hands bleeding and leg burning, collapsed in exhaustion.

CHAPTER 11

GREEN LAKE LAND STURGEON

T here it lay on the old orange tarpaulin, dead. The bloodied body of the huge lake monster was transported to the parking lot of the Leighton Township hall during the early morning hours. It was an odd location to hold a press conference, but it was a stone's throw from the lake and convenient. As the spot doubled as the town's primary fire station, it was fitting that the hub of attention was also the seat of local government.

The six parking spaces were quickly occupied, mostly by media vans. Other vehicles parked along the side of the road. The entire community turned out to gawk at the strange animal, many opting for an extra day off, as this was not a typical Monday morning. Silas Sobel,

Bonnie Jean Buckingham, Ellie Donnovan, Deputy Fischer, Fire Chief Techwyn, William Jahnke, Pham Vann, and even the guilty-looking Edgar Elzinga were among the nearly one hundred people crammed together like sardines.

"Good morning," began the man wearing the stiff, forest green uniform of the DNR. He stood at the head of the giant beast, its mouth agape, eyes locked in a death stare. "I'm Derek Brefka with the Michigan Department of Natural Resources. The reason you're all here is quite obvious. We've come into possession of the body of a previously unseen aquatic animal, taken from Green Lake by a local resident last night. I know what we see before us is shocking, and at this point there are more questions than answers.

As a precautionary measure, the lake is hereby *closed* to all public and private use until further notice. DNR and the marine patrol division of the sheriff's office will have an around-the-clock presence on the water to ensure enforcement. Scientific research teams from the department of environmental quality and environmental protection agency are en route. They'll be on site shortly to help assess the situation and provide recommendations.

Residents are advised to stay away from the water. Keep your children and pets inside for their safety. Please remain calm, but vigilant. Report any strange lake activity to our toll free tip line or on our website. Hopefully we'll have more answers for you once the marine biologists get here." Brefka stopped for a breath, and wrinkled his nose, overwhelmed by the pungent fishy smell that filled the air. "Until they arrive, we're lucky to be graced with the presence of Professor Donald Lee, part of Michigan State University's extension program. He's considered an expert on Michigan wildlife by many in his field. Any non-public safety questions may be directed to him at this time."

A man in a plaid shirt, thick glasses and wispy white mustache stepped forward from the crowd and took a stance next to Brefka.

"Hello," Lee said. "As Director Brefka indicated, I'm a professor with MSU's agricultural extension program here in the area.

What we know about this animal is very little. Some of you may recognize it as a species of fish called the Lake Sturgeon. Lake Sturgeon are also called the 'dinosaurs of the Great Lakes,' as they have been around for approximately 135 million years. It's the largest freshwater fish found in this region, and they are a threatened species. However, *this* specimen is unlike any sturgeon we've ever seen before.

Aside from its unprecedented size, another startling feature of this animal is the appearance of these extraordinarily elongated fins, which resemble limbs." The professor bent down, taking one of the arms in his hand. He worked it back and forth, causing its three curved claws to flex. "They look similar to early-stage arms and legs of young crocodiles or alligators."

Lee walked over to the creature's head, stuck his foot on the lower lip and pried up on the top of its jaws. "This young specimen was 'teething.' Although they're not visible, just under its gums here are multiple rows of serrated, predatory teeth. *Normally*, Lake Sturgeon do not have teeth." Lee stepped back, letting the sturgeon's mouth clamp shut. He wiped his hands along his pant leg and looked to the anxious media. "I'll try to answer any questions you might have."

"Ellie Donnovan, Green Lake Globe," the local journalist spoke up. All eyes went to her. "Green Lake isn't that big, about 309 acres. How can it host a massive fish like this without anyone knowing?"

"Sturgeon are natural bottom feeders, rarely seen by people. While the proportions of this one are astonishing, I'm not surprised that it's gone this long undetected."

"Why would such an ancient fish, unchanged for over a million years, suddenly sprout arms and legs?"

"I'm not sure," the professor admitted. "It could be in transitional form, going from being a marine to terrestrial-based animal."

"Does that mean it can walk on land?"

"Possibly."

"But, why?"

"Again, I'm not sure. It may be looking for a supplemental food source."

"It seems these things are suddenly and violently challenging human dominance of the area… could they be responsible for the disappearance of Billy Brush last month?"

"I'm not familiar with that particular case," Lee said. "So I can't comment." At that point, Brefka leaned forward to answer.

"We haven't seen any evidence to indicate a connection."

"Jennifer Elmore, WPLV News. Exactly *how big* is the fish?"

"This one is a staggering fifty two feet long, and weighs about four tons."

"How did it get so big?"

"We're still waiting on definitive lab results, but preliminary field tests on tissue samples have turned up positive for rBST, recombinant bovine somatotropin. It's an artificial growth hormone commonly used to make livestock bigger. It's essentially a sex steroid. It's been shown to have negative effects on fetal development in mice and humans.

Its use and disposal is tightly regulated, however unauthorized dumping of rBST-contaminated waste could explain the source of exposure. This thing could be the product of a poisoned ecosystem. If the animal started ingesting the growth hormone as a hatchling, then its transformation into a giant occurred gradually. Keep in mind that this is just pure speculation on my part. I'm not ready to jump to any conclusions at this point."

"Ron Kalvin, WWGR 15 News. We've received several reports of odd sounds heard when the animal surfaced… what was that sound?"

"From what witnesses have described, I'm guessing the sounds were what is commonly known as 'sturgeon thunder.' Normally heard in rivers and streams during spring spawning runs, the sound is usually associated with mating practices. Now it seems to be a signal for something else… another form of communication. It could signal a warning of impending aggression, like a dog growling."

"You called this a 'young specimen.' How old is it in your estimation?"

"Approximately thirty years old. It just reached sexual maturity."

"Does that mean that there are *more* of these things swimming around in Green Lake? Would the full grown adults be even *bigger?*"

"I can't say with any degree of certainty, but we have to assume that there are more of them. It's highly unlikely that this specimen is the only one like it. As for the size of any others… I don't know. There *may* be even larger ones out there."

As Professor Lee finished his answer, several official-looking government vehicles stopped in the road in front of the hall. A sleek black pickup towing a huge trailer, the letters "DEQ" stenciled on the side, lead the mini caravan. Massive RV-type vehicles marked with the seal of the EPA followed; they were topped with expensive antennas and satellites.

"That'll be all for now," Brefka announced in an authoritative voice. "Press conference is over." The DNR man paused and looked expectantly to Deputy Fisher.

"You heard the man, folks," Fischer said. "Let's move out of the area and give them some room." The crowd just stared. "Did I stutter?

Come on, let's skedaddle. Go home. Nothing left to see here."

The crowd slowly dispersed. Stragglers mingled together and started new conversations. The patient drivers of the mobile command vehicles gently edged their way forward as spaces cleared.

Professor Lee approached Silas Sobel with hand extended.

"Hello, Mr...?"

"Sobel. Silas Sobel." The vet clasped hands with the professor and pumped his arm. "Glad to meet you."

"You're the one who caught this monster...?"

"I did, with a little help from my friends. 'Monster' seems an appropriate label for that thing."

"I agree," Lee replied. "But we can't keep calling it a 'monster.' Not very scientific. It needs a proper name. You discovered them. That means you get to name them. What will it be?"

"I'm not the expert," Sobel said with raised hands. "What would you suggest?"

Professor Lee appeared to be in deep thought. He tapped his chin as his eyes wandered upward. "Let's see... these are Lake Sturgeon, found in Green Lake. They differ from known species because of their humungous size and those odd limb-fins. How about: *Medirostris Fulvescens Terre-Acipenser.* It's Latin."

"Sounds fancy, but what does it mean in English?"

"*Green Lake Land Sturgeon.*"

CHAPTER 12

DOWN IN FLAMES

"I don't like this," Sobel shook his head.

"Me neither," replied Bonnie Jean Buckingham. "Doesn't seem very smart."

"It's not," Professor Lee added excitedly. "It's stupid. And dangerous."

The trio stood on the deck behind William Jahnke's house, which overlooked the lake to the north. Although they disagreed with the plan hatched by the president of the residents' league, they still wanted to bear witness to the outcome.

After the press conference that morning, the DNR, DEQ and EPA foolishly deployed their dive teams in inflatable rubber dinghies in search of clues about the giant "land sturgeon." They didn't last an hour on the open water. When watchful residents heard the mysterious "crackle" called sturgeon thunder, many began to video record with their smart phones. They recorded the attacks in their entirety, including the last desperate screams for help by the divers. The footage was quickly posted online.

"I wish the state would send some more DNR or state troopers or something," Professor Lee said. "We've got a panicked community because of those 'viral videos.' Now everyone's in a mob mentality."

With little to no response from the authorities in the wake of the disturbing videos, the locals (led by William Jahnke) devised their own strategy. The plot to draw another monster into an ambush along the shore was improvised at best, and chronically short-sighted at worst.

"That's a hell of a bait pile," Sobel said, eyeing the mound of clams, shrimp, worms and small fish. He saw the flies swarming the pile, backlit by the setting sun.

"I hope this doesn't work," Lee opined, nervously rolling the ends of his mustache as he spoke. "If it does…"

"If it does, then we'll be ready for 'em," finished a grinning William Jahnke. The arrogant man carried his double barrel shotgun over his shoulder like a soldier on parade. "If you guys are just going to stand around, you might as well pick up a gun and help us." By "us" Jahnke referred to the dozen men, mostly seasoned hunters, who waited in semi-hidden positions around the stinking bait pile.

"No, thank you," the professor answered, crossing his arms. "I'm a scholar, not a fighter."

"If one of those monsters comes out of the water after me, then I'll blow it away," Buckingham said. "But I'm not going to stand with you and try to challenge one to a fight. You boys are asking for trouble."

"What about you, *soldier?*" Jahnke directed the question to Sobel, trying to invoke his warrior spirit. "You up to the task of protecting us?"

"There's a difference between protecting people and being irresponsible. You're taking unnecessary risks," Sobel pointed out. He narrowed his eyes at Peter Drake; the town board member held an old Winchester rifle and swayed excessively with the breeze. He was drunk again. "I can't see the wisdom of sticking our necks out there… you don't know what you're up against. You and your orange-jacket commandos have no clue what you're inviting into your own backyard, literally."

Jahnke replied with a huff and turned his back. The word "coward" was on his lips, but he didn't dare utter the insult within earshot of the Vietnam veteran. In some ways, he was more frightened by Sobel than he was of these "Green Lake Land Sturgeon."

"Good evening," called out a familiar voice. All eyes went to Deputy Fischer as he approached from the driveway.

"CJ," Jahnke nodded a greeting. "Can I help you with something?"

"What's going on back here?"

"Just a gathering of friends," Jahnke evaded. Sobel, Buckingham and Professor Lee looked on in silence from the deck.

"Looks like a gathering of *armed* friends," Fischer observed, motioning to Jahnke's shotgun. "A meeting of the Green Lake Marksmen Club?"

"No," Jahnke answered. "Just some citizens freely associating and exercising their second amendment rights. No law against open carry on private property…"

"Never said there was," Fischer sighed, frustration building. His focus went to the fly-covered heap. "Looks like you're trying to lure one of those *things* out into the open so you can use it for target practice."

"So?"

"We've got reinforcements on the way, William. We shouldn't try to handle this by ourselves. Let's all go home, hunker down and wait in place for the cavalry."

"*You* can do that, CJ, if you're so inclined. What if one of those land sturgeon come out and get into someone's house before your backup arrives? *I'm* not going to hide, or 'hunker down' while someone's wife or kids get eaten alive!"

"Going vigilante isn't the answer –"

"HUSH!" commanded a voice in a harsh whisper. It was Frank Brush, the father of the little boy who went missing a month earlier. Armed with an AR-15 rifle and a giant pistol on his hip, the man seemed overly prepared for a fight. "I think I hear something..."

CRACKLE. CRACKLE.

Thinking quickly, Sobel pushed Bonnie Jean and Professor Lee to the floor before he covered them with his own body. Everyone instantly froze, crouched down or took cover. Not a sound was heard, except for the gentle splash of water that indicated *something* coming ashore.

"Here it comes," Sobel whispered.

They watched in silence at the greenish-brown snout came out of the water, the long body pushed along by the clawed fins that were now arms. It curiously advanced, its barbels feeling everything in front of its mouth.

Once fully on land, the big fish moved forward awkwardly. Its head swept back and forth like a metal detector. Sobel noted that while this land sturgeon was no minnow, it was significantly smaller than the one he'd caught the day before.

The animal continued its search for food, moving closer to the smelly mountain. Once its whisker-barbels passed over the edge of the pile, the sturgeon sensed the presence of a meal and noisily devoured the jumble of seafood.

"LIGHTS!" Jahnke jumped up from his place of concealment,

pointing a high-lumen spotlight at the surprised creature. Holding the light with his left hand, Jahnke laid the shotgun barrel over his forearm and took a bead. The other men imitated the action, stood and took aim. The sturgeon lifted its head and innocently sniffed the air, trying to make sense of the situation. "FIRE!!"

BANG! POP! POW!

Volley after volley of varied caliber rounds struck the animal, punching holes through its body. The kinetic energy of the bullets nearly knocked the beast over, but as the ambush came from three angles, the blasts were counteracted by shots that impacted from the opposite side. The land sturgeon did a macabre, unnatural dance as it was completely riddled with lead.

BANG! POW! Click, click, click. The makeshift Green Lake militia had expended their ammunition.

"CEASE FIRE," Jahnke called out needlessly.

The land sturgeon, nearly ripped apart by the assault, feebly flopped around on the ground. An awful screech of pain combined with its unique CRACKLE rang out across the lake. Its blood flowed onto the grass. It was mortally wounded and suffering greatly.

Sobel, Buckingham and Professor Lee stood up at the same time, adjusted their clothing and brushed themselves off.

"Sorry about that," Sobel said. "Didn't mean to be so rough, but I knew the crap was about to hit the fan."

"Quite alright," Lee answered.

Bonnie Jean remained silent as she slowly descended the deck's stairs. She approached the barely-moving sturgeon and cocked her head to the side.

"Poor thing," she muttered. Silas soon appeared next to her.

"Just a baby," Sobel observed with sadness. "If the one I got was equivalent to a horny teenager, then this one's hardly a toddler."

"It just wanted something to eat," Bonnie Jean commented, wiping a tear from her eye. "It didn't do anything wrong."

"Will someone *please* put that animal out of its misery?" Professor Lee asked, his ears assaulted by the anguished cries. "I can't stand that noise."

"My pleasure," Frank Brush grunted as he brought the assault rifle to his shoulder. He pulled the trigger, but the weapon clicked harmlessly. He too had unknowingly fired every round, all thirty of them. As Brush slung the rifle and reached for his pistol, Deputy Fischer rose from his kneeling position.

"I've got it," Fischer reassured. He stood over the whimpering animal and drew his pistol.

POP! POP!

The twin shots were immediately fatal. The sturgeon lowered its head and ceased all movements.

CRACKLE. CRACKLE.

This time the sturgeon thunder didn't come from the recently killed youngster; it came from the lake and was much louder. Growing to deafening decibels, the shriek drowned out the noises of splashing water that drew near.

"RUN!" Sobel shouted as he turned and hobbled away as quickly as he could. The professor and township supervisor were hot on his heels, the others paralyzed by the shock of the situation.

The trio ran to the south, across Kalamazoo Avenue, straight toward the 3L parking lot.

SPLASH, SPLASH.

Looking over his shoulder, Sobel saw an awesome sight. A huge, lumbering land sturgeon emerged from the lake, standing on its minuscule legs as the water cascaded from its smooth skin.

"Oh my God," Bonnie Jean exclaimed, fleeing at a steady jog.

The animal was a true gargantuan – roughly eighty feet from nose to tail and it stood approximately twenty feet tall.

CRACKLE. CRACKLE.

The mammoth mouth opened and closed, sending sound waves that carried for miles. Its mouth boasted dozens of razor-sharp teeth, dripping with saliva. It dwarfed every land sturgeon seen thus far. It must be an adult. This was truly a *monster*.

Bonnie Jean, Sobel and Lee ran toward the small store, frantically calling for help. Jahnke, Fischer and the others came sprinting across the street as the giant land sturgeon gave chase. Its massive clawed foot came down on the large wooden sign that read "Welcome to Green Lake," smashing it to splintered smithereens.

Jahnke tripped over a pothole in the road, and slammed his head on the asphalt. Seconds later, the beast was on top of him. A barbel as thick as a rope brushed over his chest, and instantly decided he was food. The triangular mouth opened and inhaled the screaming man up to the waist. Jahnke squirmed and fought, but the creature clamped its jaws together, cutting the president of the residential league in half.

"Call for help!" Bonnie Jean shouted as she ran to the 3L entrance. Jesse, the clerk with the camo hat, was already on the phone. Everyone piled into the store at once; Deputy Fischer locked the door behind him.

Standing next to a gas pump, in the process of fueling his tractor with diesel fuel, was Edgar Elzinga. The old farmer who unintentionally caused all of the havoc couldn't move; he watched, slack-jawed, as the monstrous creature stomped its way toward him.

The tractor's tank started to overfill, fuel spilling onto the pavement. Seeing this, Edgar yanked the squirting nozzle out and aimed it at the approaching beast, spraying its legs, shoulders and underbelly. He dropped the handle, the fuel flow now cut off. Whispering a Hail Mary, the farmer pulled a Zippo lighter from his overalls pocket. With one flick and a toss, the colossus was instantly consumed by flames. Edgar crouched behind a large trash can, shielding his head and face from the heat.

Seconds later, the flashing red lights of the town's only fire engine pulled into the parking lot. Upon his return from responding to a routine grass fire, Chief Techwyn was shocked to see the flaming beast. He couldn't believe his eyes and immediately turned into the driveway, unsure of what he should do.

Sizzling scarlet flames licked at the animal's skin, causing it to separate and curl back. The enormous fish wavered and then fell down, succumbing to the burn. It whipped its head back and forth, emitting an angry, reverberating CRACKLE.

The fire truck's cab-mounted, high pressure water hose unleashed its powerful stream. Directed internally by the engine's driver, the nozzle swept left and right, dousing the flames. The supersized land sturgeon groaned from a prone position, its gigantic body charred black, burned flesh steaming.

"Edgar, you idiot!" Chief Techwyn shook his fist from the truck's driver seat. "You tryin' to kill us all?!"

Edgar rose from behind the trash can, grinning like a fool. "Whew! Close one!" He curiously approached the badly burned fish.

"It's still alive," Techwyn warned. "Keep back!"

As if responding on cue, the giant land sturgeon struggled to stand up. Its underdeveloped and badly burned "legs" trembled under the pressure of such weight.

Reacting to the creature's renewed efforts, Techywn accelerated and rammed the monster with the fire engine's blocky front grill. The animal screamed out, its front leg pinned beneath the truck's tire. It swung its head and slammed into the side of the truck, nearly knocking it over. The fire chief scrambled out of the vehicle and ran toward the store.

The rising noise of an earsplitting siren climbed in pitch, obscuring the thunderous sounds that came from the sturgeon's mouth. Someone across the street at the township hall/fire department activated the alarm that normally alerted residents to severe weather threats. Now it warned them of a much more dangerous menace.

Residents inquisitively stepped out of their homes or peered through windows to see what was going on. They saw the crispy lake monster immobilized by the fire truck; it took several minutes but people began to realize the monster's vulnerability.

First ten, then twenty and more locals edged their way toward the 3L property. They carried a wide array of weaponry; not only firearms but also axes, shovels, pitchforks, baseball bats… whatever was handy at the moment. Some were led by barking dogs who strained against their leashes, excited by the smell of cooked fish.

The writhing land sturgeon sensed the looming danger as the armed neighbors converged. It flapped its tail and waved its arm-fins. It tried to roll away but couldn't escape, firmly trapped by the fire truck.

One bravely drunk man was first to advance. He drew back with his heavy fiberglass-handled splitting axe and swung with all of his might. His intoxicated state meant he missed his mark, but the axe head still made contact, slicing the side of the fish. Stumbling, the man regained his footing and swung again, this time chopping deep into the monster's flank. The newly separated flesh exposed a huge white rib.

A raucous cheer went up from the crowd. They smelled blood. Emboldened by the confidence of the axe-wielding drunk, they moved in.

Recognizing the threat still posed by the injured fish, Deputy

Fischer ran from the store.

"Everyone, GET BACK!!" the deputy shouted. "It's not safe!"

The crowd, feeding off its own energy, collectively ignored the lawman. They began to bludgeon, cut, stab and shoot at the sturgeon. The beast screamed its penetrating CRACKLE with each new wound inflicted.

Professor Lee staggered into the parking lot, shocked by the brutality. He waved his arms and yelled, but like Deputy Fischer, he too was ignored.

"Get back here, professor!" Sobel yelled from the safety of the store's awning.

"Don't kill it! This is an important scientific discovery!! Don't you understand--?!"

In his attempt to reason with the irrational crowd, the professor found himself directly next to the creature.

SLASH! The sturgeon's flailing leg sprang out, its claws raked across Lee's torso, cutting him to ribbons with a single strike. The professor sank to his knees, unable to comprehend what had just happened as he bled out.

Deputy Fischer abandoned his efforts at crowd control, drew his weapon and rapidly pumped three shots into the creature's head. The fish only thrashed harder and screamed louder, the puny 9mm rounds a mere annoyance.

With a look of grim determination, Frank Brush marched over and yanked the massive hand cannon from his hip holster. He held the pistol with a double handed grip, took aim and squeezed the trigger.

BANG! The ridiculously-sized .50 caliber round hit the creature's front shoulder, blowing a huge hole in the translucent arm. The limb, still partially crushed under the truck tire, remained connected to the body by only a few slimy strands of muscle and skin. The bulky fish tried another roll, and with a "TEAR" and "SNAP," ripped the arm from its body. The torn stump continued to flex, painting the fire engine and parking lot with its blood.

SMASH! The sturgeon's oversized tail curved inward and smacked Brush with a hammer-like blow that sent him tumbling.

"Silas," Bonnie Jean elbowed Sobel's ribcage. "Look!" She pointed to the pistol lying next to the sprawled and unconscious Brush. Sobel quickly recovered the Desert Eagle before someone else could. He dodged the flapping leg-fins and tail, closing in on the creature's left side. He saw a large butcher's knife deeply embedded between the fish's ribs, pulled it out and swung it in an arc above his head. The punctured flesh held together as Sobel lifted himself up, using the knife handle for grip.

Showing incredible audacity, the veteran climbed the torso of the bucking creature, struggling to hang on. He managed to throw one leg over the beast's thick neck, straddling its head from behind. He positioned the barrel of the pistol directly over the animal's brain stem, and pulled the trigger.

BANG! BANG! BANG!

The giant pistol bucked in Sobel's hand, his wrist bending like rubber from the force of the recoil. Its skull pulverized, the creature's brain cells ceased to fire. The process took several seconds before the rest of the substantial body shut down as well. One final CRACKLE echoed from the fish's throat, dissolving into an impotent whine before silence set in. A single barbel eerily tapped the ground, a nervous reflex, as the community stared at its dying body.

Sobel, utterly fatigued, slumped to one side and slid ungracefully off the creature's neck. He hit the concrete with a thud and lay back next to his vanquished foe. Staring up at the starry night sky, he swallowed hard and clenched his eyes shut. It was finally over.

CHAPTER 13

PEOPLE WATCHING

Silas Sobel settled into his raggedy lawn chair positioned at the end of the dock. The sun shone brightly, its warming glow helped chase away the hint of a morning chill. The tension in his leg muscles gradually eased as the morning's special medicated breakfast muffin took effect.

Bending down, Sobel adjusted the volume on his old boom box, tuning to a local station. He snatched the faded green binoculars at his feet and brought them to his shade-covered eyes. Now that things had settled down, he wanted to get back to his favorite pastime and "sport;" people watching.

The people Sobel watched voyeuristically were not the typical fare. They weren't his neighbors taking out the trash, walking the dog or arguing heatedly with spouses, as he'd often witnessed. The men and women he observed wore camouflage uniforms and carried rifles.

The noise from the radio provided a soundtrack to the scenes of soldiers patrolling the lakeside roads and the lake itself. Their ridged inflatable boats and personal watercraft worked in support of the sleek trawlers marked with "EPA" and "DNR" official emblems. They were the only craft on the water at the time, a government monopoly on Green Lake.

"…the governor has declared a state of emergency in northern Allegan County," a bored-sounding newscaster read over the air. "His decision to send in the National Guard's 46th Military Police Brigade in addition to the 4th and 5th battalions of the Michigan Volunteer Defense Force is being criticized for being 'too little, too late.'

Working in conjunction with officers from the state department of natural resources and the United States Environmental Protection Agency, the troops have successfully killed or captured the remaining giant land-walking fish recently named 'Green Lake Land Sturgeon.' The abnormally-sized fish have been blamed for a string of deaths over the holiday weekend.

Residents throughout the Great Lakes region have expressed concern over other possible concentrations of genetically mutated fish. The hundreds of lakes, rivers and streams in the area will continue to be monitored for any unusual activity…"

THE END

ABOUT THE AUTHOR

Russell Slater is a freelance writer from western Michigan. His work has been published in the (Wayland) *Penasee Globe*, *Allegan County News*, Flavor 616 Magazine, Engraver's Journal, and the Volunteer: Civil Air Patrol Magazine. He lives in a rural community with his wife and son.

Contact the Author: Russell@peninsulampublishing.com

Made in the USA
Lexington, KY
20 September 2017